A Note to Parents and Caregivers:

Read-it! Readers are for children who are just starting on the amazing road to reading. These beautiful books support both the acquisition of reading skills and the love of books.

The PURPLE LEVEL presents basic topics and objects using high frequency words and simple language patterns.

The RED LEVEL presents familiar topics using common words and repeating sentence patterns.

The BLUE LEVEL presents new ideas using a larger vocabulary and varied sentence structure.

The YELLOW LEVEL presents more challenging ideas, a broad vocabulary, and wide variety in sentence structure.

The GREEN LEVEL presents more complex ideas, an extended vocabulary range, and expanded language structures.

The ORANGE LEVEL presents a wide range of ideas and concepts using challenging vocabulary and complex language structures.

When sharing a book with your child, read in short stretches, pausing often to talk about the pictures. Have your child turn the pages and point to the pictures and familiar words. And be sure to reread favorite stories or parts of stories.

There is no right or wrong way to share books with children. Find time to read with your child, and pass on the legacy of literacy.

Adria F. Klein, Ph.D.
Professor Emeritus
California State University
San Bernardino, California

Editor: Jill Kalz
Designer: Lori Bye
Page Production: Michelle Biedscheid
Art Director: Nathan Gassman
Associate Managing Editor: Christianne Jones
The illustrations in this book were created with watercolors and digitally.

Picture Window Books
151 Good Counsel Drive
P.O. Box 669
Mankato, MN 56002-0669
877-845-8392
www.picturewindowbooks.com

Library of Congress Cataloging-in-Publication Data
Meister, Cari.
King Arthur and the black knight / retold by Cari Meister ; illustrated by
Sahin Erkocak.
p. cm. — (Read-it! readers. Legends)
ISBN 978-1-4048-4834-4 (library binding)
1. Arthurian romances—Adaptations. [1. Arthur, King—Legends. 2. Knights and
knighthood—Folklore. 3. Folklore—England.] I. Erkocak, Sahin, ill. II. Title.
PZ8.1.M498Kf 2008
398.2—dc22
[E]   2008006322

King Arthur
— and the —
Black Knight

a retelling by Cari Meister
illustrated by Sahin Erkocak

Special thanks to our reading adviser:

Adria F. Klein, Ph.D.
Professor Emeritus, California State University
San Bernardino, California

PiCTURE WiNDOW BOOKS
Minneapolis, Minnesota

"Merlin," said King Arthur, "there is peace in the kingdom of Camelot. There are no battles to fight. Let's go for a ride in the woods."

The horses clicked along the castle road. Soon they reached the edge of the woods. Arthur flipped down the visor on his helmet.

"Let's race," said Arthur. "First man to reach the oak tree wins!"

King Arthur was fit and strong. He was fast on his horse. But Merlin always won. He used magic to win!

On this day, however, the race took a different turn.

In the middle of the path stood a knight dressed in black.

"Turn back or fight," said the black knight.

Arthur didn't like to fight for no reason. But the black knight wouldn't move. He didn't know it was King Arthur under the visor.

"If you insist," said Arthur.

The men charged. They rode fast and hard. Their wooden lances broke.

The men got off their horses. They drew their swords. The black knight was bigger than Arthur and very strong. Arthur was quick on his feet and fast with his sword.

The two men fought for hours. Then, the black knight struck a mighty blow. Arthur's sword broke in two.

"You are a strong fighter," said the black knight.
"But now you have no weapon. Give up."

"Never," said Arthur.

Just then, Merlin stepped from the trees and touched the black knight. The knight quickly fell to the ground.

"Is he dead?" asked Arthur.

"No. He is sleeping," said Merlin. "Don't worry about him. We must care for your wounds. You are hurt!"

After three days, Arthur was well again.

"Merlin," said Arthur, "the black knight broke my sword. I need a new one."

"Follow me," said Merlin.

Merlin and Arthur rode for days. Late one night, they came to a glowing lake.

"Look!" said Merlin.

In the middle of the lake, a long white arm held up a sword. The sword had a jewel on the hilt. Jewels covered the scabbard, or sheath, too.

"The sword is called Excalibur," said Merlin. "It belongs to her." Merlin pointed to a lady dressed in green.

The woman stepped from the mist. "I am the Lady of the Lake," she said. "I have been waiting for you. You may borrow my sword. But you must use it only for good."

On the way back to Camelot, Merlin asked Arthur, "Which do you think is better, the sword or the scabbard?"

"The sword," said Arthur.

"The sword is very fine," said Merlin, "but the scabbard is magical. As long as you wear the scabbard, you will not lose a drop of blood."

Soon Merlin and Arthur were back at the oak tree. Once again, the black knight stood in the middle of the path.

"You are back!" he said. "Ready to fight again?"

"If you insist," said Arthur.

The men's swords clinked and clashed. The black knight was stronger than ever.

The battle went on and on. Blood dripped from the black knight. But Arthur wore the magical scabbard. No blood fell from his body.

Finally, the black knight dropped to the ground. "Please, sir," he said. "Don't kill me."

"I will let you live," said Arthur, raising his visor. "But you must promise to serve my kingdom."

"King Arthur!" said the black knight. "I didn't know it was you! Thank you for sparing my life."

The black knight never drew his sword on
strangers again. He served King Arthur for
the rest of his life.

More *Read-it!* Readers

Bright pictures and fun stories help you practice your reading skills. Look for more books at your level.

How Spirit Dog Made the Milky Way:
   A Retelling of a Cherokee Legend
King Arthur and the Black Knight
King Arthur and the Sword in the Stone
Mato the Bear and Devil's Tower:
   A Retelling of a Lakota Legend
Robin Hood and the Golden Arrow
Robin Hood and the Tricky Butcher

On the Web

FactHound offers a safe, fun way to find Web sites related to topics in this book. All of the sites on FactHound have been researched by our staff.

1. Visit *www.facthound.com*

2. Type in this special code:
   1404848347

3. Click on the FETCH IT button.

Your trusty FactHound will fetch the best sites for you!
A complete list of *Read-it!* Readers is available on our Web site:
www.picturewindowbooks.com